The Sock Princess

Written and Illustrated by Julie Thorpe

AuthorHouse™
1663 Liberty Drive
Bloomington, IN 47403
www.authorhouse.com
Phone: 1 (800) 839-8640

Published by AuthorHouse 09/25/2015

ISBN: 978-1-5049-5018-3 (sc)
ISBN: 978-1-5049-5017-6 (e)

Library of Congress Control Number: 2015915232

Print information available on the last page.

This book is printed on acid-free paper.

authorHOUSE®

Dedication

This book is dedicated to my family,
for their love and encouragement,
to future grandchildren,
and to all the Sock Princesses out there,
including my own.

I know a girl, maybe you know her too,
There could be a sock princess somewhere near you.
She drives her mom crazy each day that goes by.
Her socks are the problem...read on and learn why.

"Hurry up, Emily!" her mother would say.
Mornings weren't Emily's best time of day.
Now, choosing her socks was a really big chore,
So her mother pulled out some white
socks from her drawer.

Emily looked at the socks, then looked down.
She didn't like socks that were white, black or brown.
Her favorite socks were the ones with red dots.
She wore those ones often, she liked those ones lots.

"Emily, Emily, I'll count to three –
Put those socks on just as quick as can be!"
But her mother had seen the sock problem before
She knew it could take 20 minutes – or MORE!

The socks she liked best were no longer clean,
They had to be washed in the washing machine.
So she opened her drawer and looked all around,
And finally socks with cool colors were found.

Emily dressed from her head to her toe,
Ate breakfast, washed up and was ready to go.
As her family got ready to head out the door,
Emily threw off her socks on the floor.

"Emily, Emily, I'll count to three –
Put those socks on just as quick as can be!"
But her mother had seen the sock problem before
She knew it could take 20 minutes – or MORE!

Her mom watched as Emily reached up inside,
Pulled the sock inside-out, and then she replied,
"My socks are all lumpy, and bumpy in there,
I don't like the feeling inside of this pair."

With her fingers she pulled off a few bits of fluff
"I'll be ready as soon as I take out this stuff."
Turning the socks back from outside to in,
She pulled them on slowly and started to grin.

9

Do you think she was ready to get in the car?
She reached for her boots, but she didn't get far.
With a frown on her face she sat down with a bump.
"I can't go yet, Mommy, my sock has a lump."

The socks had a bumpy seam over her toes
So off they did come as she wrinkled her nose.
"Emily, Emily, I'll count to three –
Put those socks on just as quick as can be!"

Her mother sat down and let out a sigh,
As Emily then pulled the socks back up high.
"That's better, Mommy, they're on nice and straight.
We'd better be going or we might be late."

She was ready to get on her coat and boots when
Emily pulled off her socks once again!
These socks were too big, they bunched up at her heel
"Mommy, I don't like the way these socks feel."

"Emily, Emily, I'll count to three –
Put those socks on just as quick as can be!"
'Though her mother had seen the sock problem before,
They didn't **have** 20 minutes or more!

Now Emily's dad knew the sock problem, too,
And he'd waited calmly, he knew what to do.
He went to the laundry, and 'though they weren't clean,
He pulled the right socks from the washing machine.

"Here my sock princess," said dad with a wink,
"That's what we should have done first, don't you think?"
So, with many more minutes then 20 now past
This little sock princess was ready – AT LAST!

They jumped in the car, did their seatbelts up tight
But wait, suddenly there was something not right…
'Thump, thump", could be heard, and in the back seat
Emily was once again in bare feet.

"Oh Emily, Emily," mother did scold,
Put your boots on before you get cold!"
"It's okay, Mommy, my feet were too hot.
I don't need any socks in these boots that I've got."

Her mommy and dad didn't know what to say,
They just hoped that at last they could be on their way.

In the end, they all learned that the right socks for play
Are the ones that look good and feel just the right way.
Now, maybe you know her, it could be quite true,
There could be a sock princess somewhere near you.

CPSIA information can be obtained
at www.ICGtesting.com
Printed in the USA
LVIC06n0517131115
462345LV00005B/20

* 9 7 8 1 5 0 4 9 5 0 1 8 3 *